DOUBLES
TROUBLES

DOUBLES
TROUBLES

Betty Hicks

Illustrated by Simon Gane

ROARING BROOK PRESS
NEW YORK

Many thanks to expert tennis player Tarina Herb for reading my manuscript and confirming the accuracy of my tennis knowledge.

And, an extra thank-you to Smedes Lindner, who inadvertantly gave me the idea for this series when she couldn't find enough sports books for early readers.—B.H.

Cataloging-in-Publication Data is on file at the Library of Congress
Hicks, Betty.
ISBN: 978-1-59643-489-9

Roaring Brook Press books are available for special promotions and premiums.
For details, contact: Director of Special Markets, Holtzbrinck Publishers.

Book design by Jennifer Browne
Printed in April 2010 in the United States of America
by Worzalla, Stevens Point, Wisconsin
First edition May 2010
2 4 6 8 10 9 7 5 3 1

For John Drake

CONTENTS

BLAP!

Henry stood three feet back from the net, his tennis racket raised and ready. He pictured Rocky behind him—getting ready to serve.

Right now, thought Henry, Rocky's taking a deep breath. And *now*, he's swinging his racket back with one arm and tossing the ball up with the other.

Henry listened for the *thwack* of Rocky's racket hitting the ball. *What was taking him so long?*

They *had* to win this point or they'd lose their doubles match. Too many losses meant no trophy. Henry loved trophies. Even more, Henry loved playing.

Just thinking that the match might end so soon made Henry grind his teeth.

Thwack! Rocky finally hit his serve. *Blap!* The ball hit the tape on the top of the net and fell at Henry's feet. Rocky had missed his first serve.

"Hey!" cried Henry. "Don't worry about it."

After all, a server gets *two* chances to put the ball in play. But if Rocky messed up again, that would be a double fault—and they'd lose the point. End of game, set, and match.

Henry turned to Rocky and pumped his fist in support. "You can do it!"

Rocky clenched his jaw and nodded. He bounced the ball hard, getting ready for his second serve. Match point. Last chance.

Henry turned back to face the net. He stared down the kid who was crouched on the other side, ready to receive Rocky's serve.

"Come on, Rocky," Henry whispered, "ace him."

Secretly, Henry wished it were *his* turn to serve. Henry's serve was the best part of his game. On a good day, he could hit the ball so hard and aim it so well, no one could touch it—a perfect ace. And, Henry never double faulted.

Not that Rocky was a *bad* tennis player. He just wasn't as good as Henry.

Blap! Rocky's serve struck the net again. The ball dropped down and rolled the length of the net. Henry stared after it as if it were a big yellow bug looking for a place to hide. Stupid ball, thought Henry.

Henry and Rocky had lost their match.

PARTNERS

Goose, Rita, and Jazz surrounded Henry and Rocky after the match.

"Too bad." "You'll win next time." "Those guys were good," they all said at once.

Goose, Rita, Jazz, Rocky, and Henry were friends

who lived in the same neighborhood. They had exactly enough people for a basketball team, or anything else they wanted to play. Which was perfect because they all loved sports—especially Henry.

Henry was glad they were trying to make him feel better.

"Those guys *were* good," Henry agreed. "Too good for me." Which was a lie, but he didn't want Rocky to feel any worse than he already did. After all, Rocky *had* lost the match.

"What you need," said Rocky, "is a new partner. I stink."

"You do not," said Jazz.

Goose held his nose. "Yeah, he does. He smells like monster sweat."

Rita jabbed Goose.

"Ow," said Goose, rubbing his arm. Rita could throw a punch like a prizefighter.

"Hey!" Henry exclaimed. "I don't want somebody else!"

But even as he said it, he knew that just ten minutes ago he'd wished Goose were his doubles partner

instead of Rocky. Goose had a better serve than Rocky, *and* he had a better backhand. Not only that, but his long arms could reach lobs—those high, arcing balls that sailed way over your head. Goose could put those away with an overhead smash that made Henry's jaw drop.

But Coach had paired Goose with another player.

And Henry would never suggest a switch. That would make Rocky feel like dirt.

"Just work on your serve before the next match," Rita advised Rocky.

And your backhand, Henry thought.

Goose pulled a Tootsie Pop out of his pocket. It had so much lint on it that Henry couldn't even guess what flavor it was.

"Eeew," said Rita.

Goose handed the lollipop to Rocky.

"Thanks!" said Rocky. He picked some of the lint off with his fingers; then he popped the whole thing into his mouth.

"Do you have any more?" Henry asked.

"Nope," said Goose, pulling his empty pockets inside out. "Sorry."

Jazz tugged Rocky's hand and said, "Come on. You must be thirsty. Let's get you some Gatorade."

"Then let's look for an open court," said Rita. "We'll help you practice your serve."

The next thing Henry knew, all his friends were walking away. Rita was offering Rocky some of her lemon drops. Goose had one long arm draped over Rocky's shoulder. Jazz still held on to Rocky's hand.

Henry wanted to yell, "Hey! What about me? I lost too!"

Instead, he ran to catch up.

ROTTEN RETURNS

A week later, Henry's dad dropped Rocky and Henry at their next match.

Rocky had spent the entire week practicing his serve until it was awesome. Rocky never gave up on anything. Henry felt stupid for ever wanting a new partner.

"Race you!" shouted Henry, and took off running for the court.

Rocky sprinted right beside him.

They reached the court at the same time.

"Time for warm-ups!" shouted Coach.

Rocky and Henry trotted onto the court. They stretched. Then they began their first drill, side-stepping back and forth from the baseline to the net. They kept their backs straight and their weight forward.

"How many times did Coach say we had to do this?" asked Henry.

"Six," said Rocky.

"How many times do we have left?

"Two."

"No way," said Henry. It seemed as if he'd already done ten.

When they finished the drill, they both slurped water from their water bottles. Henry squirted Rocky. Rocky squirted him back. They laughed.

Henry couldn't wait for the game to start.

"See those guys?" Henry tilted his head at the two kids they were about to play. Both of them were running up to the net and touching the ground with their hands, then scurrying back, backward. One kid tripped and fell.

"We'll destroy them," said Rocky.

Henry bumped fists with Rocky.

Rocky served first. He slammed an ace right past the kid who had tripped.

"Fifteen–love," said Rocky, announcing the score.

Henry gave him a thumbs-up.

No matter how many times he heard it, Henry thought tennis scoring was weird. *Love* meant zero, and the first point scored was called fifteen instead of one. The second point was thirty. Then forty. If the score was tied *at* forty, it was called deuce. But if it was tied *before* forty, it was called *all*—so you had to say "fifteen–all" or "thirty–all." Whoever dreamed up all that must have been goofier than Goose—or rotten at math.

Rocky's next serve was good, but the other kid returned it deep, straight to Rocky's backhand. In one motion, Rocky turned his body to the left so that the back of the hand holding the racket faced the ball.

Henry held his breath. He knew a backhand shot was tough for Rocky. He was better at hitting forehand strokes—when his palm faced the ball.

Rocky just barely got a racket on it and sent the ball sideways.

"Fifteen–all," said Rocky. He took a deep breath and got ready to serve again.

He aced it.

"Thirty–fifteen."

But then he lost the next point because he hit another rotten backhand.

"Thirty–all."

It wasn't Rocky's fault, but Henry felt as if he might as well be sitting at a movie somewhere, eating popcorn. He hadn't gotten near the ball!

But the next return shot came straight at him. Henry smashed it between the two players for a point. "Yes!" cried Henry.

On the next rally, one kid rushed the net and hit a drop shot that Henry had to dive for, but he reached it. Then the other kid drilled it right back to Rocky's backhand.

Rocky missed.

The score was tied at forty.

"Deuce," said Rocky, announcing the score.

His next two serves were good, but the two kids on the other side of the net hit everything straight back to Rocky's backhand. And Rocky missed.

He and Henry lost the first game of the first set.

"They're better than they look," Rocky muttered to Henry.

"No kidding," said Henry. "Er . . . Rocky. I think they figured out that your backhand. . . uh . . . uh . . ."

"Stinks?" said Rocky.

"Needs work," said Henry.

"Well, duh," said Rocky.

"But your serve was awesome!" said Henry.

"Yeah," Rocky muttered. "Right."

Henry knew what Rocky was thinking—that they were about to lose again. Because of Rocky's rotten backhand. Henry was afraid he might be right.

JAZZ TO THE RESCUE

Henry sat on his bed, hugging his knees to his chest. He stared at all the trophies he'd won—baseball, basketball, swimming, soccer, track, singles tennis, you name it. Everything except doubles tennis. Henry slumped. He would *never* have a doubles tennis trophy. He and Rocky had lost their match. Again.

It wasn't fair! Henry was good. He could beat anybody! If only Rocky weren't his partner.

But what could he do? Cover the whole court?

No—everyone would call him a hot dog for hogging the ball.

Quit?

N'uh-uh—he wanted to play even more than he wanted a trophy.

Ask Coach for a new partner and hurt Rocky's feelings?

Nope—Rocky was his friend.

Miss a bunch of shots so losing would be both their faults?

What? No way. That was so crazy Henry couldn't believe his brain had thought it.

Henry flopped back against his pillow. He stared at his wall calendar and wished it were soccer season.

"Henry!" called his mom. "Jazz is here."

Henry sat up. Jazz would know what to do!

Henry leaped down the stairs three at a time and skidded into the den.

Jazz stood holding a mountain of books that was almost taller than she was. Henry could see only the top of her head. She began to pile them on the coffee table.

"Ready?" she asked, smiling proudly at the stack.

"For what?" asked Henry.

Jazz laughed. "You're kidding, right?"

Henry's brain went blank. What was he supposed to be ready for?

"Henry," said Jazz, using her patient voice, "we have a History project. Remember?"

History. Henry tried to push tennis and Rocky out of his mind to make room for History. Then it hit him! *Explorers.* They were doing a unit on early explorers. His teacher, Mrs. Matthews, had paired him with Jazz.

How could he forget? Getting Jazz as a partner for a school project was about as lucky as a guy could get. Jazz made straight A's. Not only that, but she knew stuff.

"Right!" said Henry. "History."

Jazz sighed with relief. "I got some books from the library."

Henry couldn't believe anyone checked out books from the library anymore. Why didn't she just look everything up on the Internet?

Jazz began opening books to the pages she'd marked with Post-it notes. She pointed to one. "Look. Here's a picture of the first fort at Jamestown. We could build a model of it."

Jazz pushed that book toward Henry and reached for another one. "Here's one on the Lost Colony. We could write a skit. Can you draw maps? We'll need a

summary report. And charts. Do you have any pictures of Croatan Indians?"

Whoa! thought Henry. *Slow down.* His brain was still working on the part about the fort—the one at Jamestown.

"So." Jazz spread her arms wide in front of the scattered books. "What do you think?"

Henry gaped. What did he think?

He thought he'd rather play tennis.

I'D RATHER EAT ROCKS

As soon as Jazz left, Henry took off for Rocky's house. He heard thumps. Was Rocky's dad building something?

No. Rocky was in his driveway, hitting backhand shots against his garage door.

"How's it going?" asked Henry.

"Not so hot," said Rocky.

Thwack! Rocky hit the ball.

Thump! The ball smacked the garage door.

Bump! It bounced back toward Rocky's backhand.

Blap! Rocky whacked it sideways into his neighbor's yard.

"Want some help?"

"Not now," said Rocky. "I've got to start my History project."

"Man," Henry said with a groan. "I'd rather eat rocks. Who's your partner?"

"Rita," said Rocky. "She's going to do a Native American dance like the tribe that Columbus met when he landed in America. And I'm going to draw pictures of how they dressed."

"Oh," said Henry. The word slumped out of his mouth sounding small and sad. What could *he* do?

Henry trudged home and went to his room. He didn't want to think about his project. Instead, he stared at his trophies. He pushed them closer together to make room for one more. He pictured *First Place, Doubles Tennis* sitting there.

Then he pictured the backhand shot that Rocky had just sent sailing in the wrong direction.

Well . . . Rocky *was* practicing. Maybe he'd get better. Maybe they could still win the tournament. Maybe frogs could fly.

HENRY'S PLAN

Henry sat at the desk in his room. He chewed on his pencil eraser and tried to think of ideas for his History project. Jazz had left him all her books and asked him to pick a topic that he liked.

Should he make a list? Once, he had made a practice schedule for Goose to work on his goalie skills. But that was for sports. Henry had never made a list of school ideas in his life, but he'd seen Jazz make a lot of them. Maybe that would help. He wrote:

1. The Lost Colony

But what about it? thought Henry. He wasn't even sure what state it was in. Virginia? North Carolina? South Carolina? It was lost, right?

2. Croatan Indians

They had hung out around the Lost Colony. But what about them? Did they play tennis?

Tennis. Henry chewed on his eraser some more. What could Henry do to help Rocky play better? Nothing. Rocky was already working as hard as he could.

Besides, they'd lost two matches. It was probably too late to win a trophy. Did Henry really need a trophy? No. He just wanted to play well and have fun and eat pizza with the team at the end of the season.

Henry pulled out a clean piece of paper. He made a new list—about tennis and what he should do.

1. Have fun
2. Play my best
3. Try not to make Rocky feel bad

Henry smiled at his list, happy to have a plan.

The next day, when Henry showed up at practice, he was still happy. His plan felt right. He was *not* going to worry about losing anymore.

Then he saw Coach's win–lose chart.

"See this?" said Coach. He held up a graph that showed everyone's matches.

There were five doubles pairs playing on Coach's team. The pair who won the most matches against the other half of the rec league would win a trophy. Rocky and Henry had lost two matches. Goose and his partner had won two matches. The other three pairs had each won one, lost one.

Everyone had four matches left to play.

"I'm showing you this," said Coach, "so you can see that anyone can still win the trophy." He clenched his fist and said, "Practice. Play hard. Don't give up."

Henry looked at Rocky.

Rocky had that look on his face—the stubborn one that said, "I never give up."

Henry grinned. Then he tried to undo it. He forced his smile muscles down. After all, he had a plan, and it didn't include winning. *Right?*

"And," said Coach, "the winner will go on to play the winner of another rec league."

Whoa, thought Henry. We'd get to play the best kids in town.

All through practice, Henry kept an eye on Coach. He was helping Rocky with his backhand.

"You're shifting your weight too soon," Coach told Rocky. "Keep your weight on your left foot longer. And keep your eye on the ball."

Rocky hit four solid backhands in a row before he missed the fifth.

Henry's heart beat faster. He *did* want to win. And it looked like he had a chance.

7

SOLID, STRONG, BORING

When Henry and Rocky showed up to play their next match, Henry's I-don't-care-if-I-win plan was history.

Henry had tried not to get his hopes up. He really had. But all week he heard Rocky hitting tennis balls against his garage.

Thwack! Thump! Bump! Thwack! Over and over again.

Rocky's backhand was so much better—they *could* win!

Plus, Coach had helped them work out a plan that was sheer genius.

"The best doubles teams," said Coach, "know their strengths and weaknesses. They work as a team. Rocky, now that your backhand's better, you and Henry both have pretty solid ground strokes. You're stronger at that than you are at hitting at the net. So,

I want you *both* to play back. Don't rush the net. Just keep the ball in play. Wait for the other team to make a mistake."

Henry and Rocky locked their arms into a two-man huddle.

"We're going to win!" exclaimed Henry.

"Yeah!" cried Rocky.

Henry received the first serve and returned it deep. Rocky moved to the back of the court with Henry. Their opponent—a kid with a million freckles—hit it straight to Rocky's backhand. Rocky returned it. For a second, Rocky looked surprised. Then he choked back a laugh. It came out sounding like a happy hiccup.

Freckle Kid and his tall partner both rushed the net. Tall Guy slammed it back.

Henry reached the ball and lobbed it over both their heads.

Love–fifteen. Rocky and Henry were off to a good start. To win the match, they had to win two out of three sets.

Tall Guy and Freckle Kid kept trying fancy stuff. Rushing the net. Overhead slams. Trying to place the ball as close to the outside line as they could. When it worked, not even Henry could return it. But most of the time they missed.

Rocky and Henry just kept hitting it back. The same ground shots—over and over and over again. Solid, strong, and basically boring. But who cared? It worked!

Rocky missed a few backhands. And he double-faulted twice. But he and Henry won anyway. Two sets and the match!

"Woo-hoo!" cried Rita when it was over. She twirled on one toe, then high-fived both of them.

"See!" Jazz said to Rocky. "I told you that you don't stink!"

Rocky made a big deal out of sniffing his armpit and grinning.

"Eeew," said Rita.

Rocky and Henry cracked up.

"So," said Jazz, turning to Henry and changing the subject. "When can we work on our History project?"

"Later," said Henry. He couldn't wait until his next match.

HENRY'S BEST

Henry heard his doorbell. He knew exactly who was ringing it.

It *had* to be Jazz—ready to begin their History project.

Henry knew he had to start it. Jazz was counting on him.

Henry didn't hate schoolwork. There were just so many other things he'd rather do. Like play tennis. Or basketball. Or eat waffles. Watch TV. Play computer games. Sleep. Clean his room. Count blades of grass.

Henry answered the door.

"Hi, Henry," said Jazz. "Ready?"

"Yeah," Henry lied.

"Did you look at the books I left you?"

"Yeah," Henry lied again.

"What'd you decide?" asked Jazz.

"Decide?" asked Henry.

"What subject do you want to do?" asked Jazz.

"Uh . . . I think you should pick," said Henry.

"Okay. Let's do the Lost Colony. You be James the First, King of England," said Jazz. "And I'll be your advisor. You ask me what happened to the Lost Colony that vanished when Elizabeth was queen. Then I'll give you a report on what went wrong—so *you* can do it right."

"That's it?" said Henry. "I just stand up in front of the class and ask what went wrong, and you do all the work? Cool."

Jazz made a face at Henry. "You *will* have to dress

like a king. And make a poster board with pictures and stuff. But I'll write up the report and do everything else. Okay?"

"Sure," said Henry. He knew a good deal when he heard it.

"I *really* want to do well," said Jazz. "I got a B+ on our last History test, and this project is my best chance to bring my grade back up to an A."

Henry nodded. He'd gotten a C+. With Jazz's help, maybe he could bring *his* grade up to a B. "I'll do my best," he answered.

After Jazz left, Henry went online to look for pictures of the Lost Colony. He found a bunch of maps. But no matter what he typed in the search box, he couldn't find any pictures of the Indians or the settlers or their village.

I've been doing this for an hour! he thought. Where's the good stuff? Okay, he knew it was way before cameras were invented, but how about a painting? Or a pencil sketch? And then it hit him. The colony was lost, so—duh—nobody knew what it looked like.

"Oh, man," he groaned, "this is going to be hard."

For one whole week, Henry practiced tennis and worked on his history project.

On Monday, he hit backhand shots to Rocky in his driveway. *Thwack!* Bounce. *Thwack!* Bounce. Rocky returned almost all of them. Then Henry went home and downloaded all the Lost Colony maps he'd found on the Internet.

Tuesday, Henry went to practice. He and Rocky worked on their ground strokes. Coach made them stand at the baseline and hit twenty balls in a row to each other.

"If either of you miss," said Coach, "you have to start over."

Henry rolled his head around twice and moaned. But secretly, he thought it would be fun.

After practice he went home and toasted a waffle

for a snack. Then he climbed into his attic looking for
anything useful for his History project. Sitting cross-
legged, he rummaged through a box filled with old
National Geographic magazines. He flipped through
a million pages and thought about tennis.

The attic was hot and the books were dusty. Henry
sweated. He sneezed. He muttered some bad words
that he wasn't allowed to say.

And then he found it! One whole issue on the Lost
Colony and what it *might* have looked like! There

were drawings of settlers, villages, cooking pots, ships, tools—you name it!

It rained so hard on Wednesday, Henry couldn't play tennis. Instead, he cut out all the pictures he'd found. He had trouble cutting straight lines because his scissors were dull. But when he finished, the pictures didn't look too bad.

On Thursday, he ran straight to Rocky's house after school. Rocky hit lobs to him so Henry could perfect his overhead smash. *Whap!* Henry walloped Rocky's lobs so hard they bounced onto the roof and rolled into the gutter—where they stayed. Henry loved hitting overhead smashes, but he had to quit because all their balls were stuck.

Henry trudged home and pasted his Lost Colony maps and pictures onto a big poster board. He was tired, but still, he did his best to line them up straight. He tried even harder to make his captions neat.

Friday, Coach helped him rotate his shoulders and hips together for more power. Henry loved power. It reminded him of overhead smashes. Meanwhile, Rocky hit backhand shots until they looked almost easy. "You're awesome!" Henry pounded him on the back.

Then he went home and worked on his king costume. He cut a crown out of yellow paper and stapled it into a circle that fit his head. He looked in the mirror.

Henry looked like a king. He felt like a king. His History project was done! And tomorrow he and Rocky were going to win their next tennis match!

MATCH POINT

Before the match, Henry strolled up to Rocky and said, "What's up?"—as if his insides weren't lobbing his heart back and forth between his ribs. As if winning didn't matter.

Henry didn't want to freak Rocky out with too much pressure. But Henry wanted to win so badly, he could taste it. It tasted half sweet, like maple syrup. But it also tasted half gross, like metal on his tongue.

Henry checked out Coach's graph. Goose was still undefeated—he and his partner had won three matches. Rocky and Henry had won one and lost two. They would have to win every match to have a shot at a trophy *and* the chance to play the kids in the other league.

"Those guys are undefeated," said Rocky, pointing across the net to their opponents.

Henry saw a kid hitting lob shots—some of them landed out of bounds. The other kid was practicing drop shots, but not all of them cleared the net.

They don't look all *that* great, thought Henry. "We can beat them," he declared.

Rocky bounced up and down on his toes, shifting his weight back and forth. "Let's do it," he said.

Henry served first. An ace!

"Yes!" cried Rocky.

Henry's next serve crossed the net like a bullet. It *felt* like an ace. But the boy who had been practicing lob shots fired it back. *Whoa!* Henry had never seen a ball come back so fast. He just barely managed to return it. Then the kid who'd been hitting drop shots rushed the net and hit an over-head slam that landed at Rocky's feet. It hit the court and soared up like a rocket launched to the moon.

Man, thought Henry. They play better than they practice.

Rocky looked at Henry and said, "Uh-oh."

"We can do this!" Henry hissed back.

The score was tied. "Deuce." "Deuce." "Deuce." Over and over again.

Henry wiped sweat off his neck and worried—this is *one* game. We have to win *lots* of games just to win a set, and then two sets out of three to win a match. We could be here forever!

But they won. Finally.

Then, it was Lob Boy's turn to serve. Henry returned it, but Rocky missed his next shot.

Henry and Rocky played back like Coach had told them—waiting for the other side to make a mistake.

But Lob Boy and the Drop-Shot Kid didn't make mistakes. They were like robots. They returned everything.

"Look for their weakness," said Coach.

"They don't have one," groaned Henry.

Somehow, Henry figured out a way to return most of their shots. But Rocky didn't.

"I'm sorry," said Rocky.

"Relax. It's okay," answered Henry. Except his brain was saying, *It's not fair. I'm playing awesome, and I'm losing.*

Rocky and Henry may have won the first game, but they lost the set. The only weakness anywhere on the court was Rocky.

Henry knew it. Rocky knew it. And the superstars on the other side of the net knew it—big-time.

The match was two sets out of three. If Rocky and Henry lost the next set, the match was over.

Lob Boy and his buddy tried to hit everything straight to Rocky. Henry ran until he thought his legs would drop off. Even though Coach had said not to,

Henry rushed the net and volleyed. He dropped back and rallied. He covered his side of the court plus half of Rocky's.

"I've got it!" called Rocky.

Henry rushed over, making Rocky move out of the way.

Rocky clenched his fists. Henry knew Rocky was getting mad, but he couldn't let them lose. He just couldn't.

Rocky and Henry's match took longer than anyone's. All the other matches were over. Everyone was watching *them*.

Rita, Goose, and Jazz shouted, "Go Rocky! Come on Henry! You can do it!"

The set was at match point, and it was Henry's serve. Henry announced the score. If he lost *this* point, it was over. Game, set, match—everything.

The Drop-Shot Kid returned Henry's serve. Henry rushed the net and slammed it back—a perfect put-away. But somehow, Lob Boy reached it. He lobbed it over Henry's head. Henry turned to run back.

"I've got it!" called Rocky.

Henry looked. The ball was headed for Rocky's backhand, but it was an easy get. Rocky could return it. No sweat.

Rocky planted his feet just right. He swung low at the ball. *Thwack!* The ball rose toward the net. It smacked the tape. *Blap!* It dropped at Henry's feet.

"No!" Henry shouted at Rocky. "You idiot!"

As soon as the words flew out of Henry's mouth, he wanted to take them back.

My Stuff Stinks

Jazz tugged Rocky's hand, and said, "Come on. You need a Gatorade."

"Here," said Rita. "Have a lemon drop."

"You did your best," said Goose, patting down the pockets of his tennis shorts.

He seemed to be looking for a Tootsie Pop for Rocky.

Henry watched all his friends walk away. Each one of them turned and shot him a dirty look.

Henry slumped onto the nearest bench. He knew he'd blown it. How could he have yelled at Rocky?

I'm the idiot, thought Henry.

But still, Rocky did *not* do his best. He missed an easy shot. Anybody could have returned it!

It wasn't fair.

Henry spent all day Sunday at home—alone. He shot some hoops in his driveway. He hoped his friends would hear the ball bouncing and come over.

They didn't.

Henry wished he hadn't yelled at Rocky. But he didn't know how to undo it.

He could tell Rocky he was sorry, but then what? He'd have to say something nice like, *You played great*. But Rocky *hadn't* played great. He had stunk.

Well, thought Henry, *they can't stay mad at me forever*. On Monday, Jazz will see my half of our History project. It's so awesome, she'll forget all about me yelling at Rocky. Right?

On Monday, Henry carried his project into class. Proudly, he propped his poster board up on the display table. He slipped his paper crown onto his head. He forced his smile muscles to turn down—he didn't want to act like a hotshot just because he'd done a great job.

Henry glanced around at the other projects. His pictures were better. Weren't they? Well . . . now that he really studied them, his pictures didn't look quite as good as he'd thought.

Henry tugged on a couple of crooked ones and tried to straighten them. He wished he'd found sharper scissors to cut them with. How had everyone else made their edges so smooth?

And look at their captions! Did they use stencils?

Henry hurried over to help Jazz carry her stuff.

She acted as if she didn't see him.

"Come on, Jazz. Give me a break. I'm sorry I yelled at Rocky."

"Look," said Jazz. "It's not his fault he's not as good as you."

Huh? thought Henry. What did that have to do with anything?

Jazz stared at Henry's paper crown.

"Hey!" said Henry. "Let's see your project."

He helped her lift a box onto the table. *Wow!* thought Henry.

Jazz's eyes sparkled as she uncovered a perfect copy of a Croatan village made out of sticks and fabric scraps. It looked as if a grown-up had built it. Then Jazz set up a chart labeled, *The Lost Colony History Mystery*. It listed a dozen ideas about what could have happened to the Lost Colony. It looked as if a sign-making company had made it. Plus, she had a stack of note cards ready, filled with her advice to King James.

Henry touched the top of his head to make sure his crown was on straight.

Jazz reached into a duffel bag and pulled out her costume. She swung a soft, thick cape around her shoulders, then topped it off with a giant white collar that was pleated like a fan. She puffed out her pants legs and tugged her socks up over the bottoms to make them look like old-timey pants. Then she clipped gold buckles to the tops of her shoes.

Henry jerked the paper crown off his head. He crumpled it into a big yellow wad.

Rita danced her way into the classroom wearing beads around her neck and a buckskin dress with fringe. Rocky set up his drawings on an easel.

"Rocky!" exclaimed Henry. "Those are awesome!"

And they were. A famous artist couldn't have done
better.

Rocky turned away.

All of a sudden, Henry wished he could go home.
Rocky's feelings were still hurt—because of him.
And he was pretty sure that his and Jazz's project

51

wasn't going to get an A—also because of him.

Henry noticed Jazz looking at his poster board. He watched the sparkle in her eyes fade. Her body slumped. Henry thought if bodies could talk, hers was screaming, *This is not fair!*

"Jazz," whispered Henry. "I'm really sorry. My stuff stinks!"

He watched her stand tall and pretend it was okay.

Henry felt awful. But it wasn't his fault! He had totally done his best. He had spent more time on this project than on any homework he had ever done in his life.

Jazz was just a better student. No matter how hard Henry tried, he would never be as good as her.

Wait. Didn't Jazz just say the same thing about Rocky's tennis? That it wasn't Rocky's fault he wasn't as good as Henry?

Oh, thought Henry.

FRIENDS

Henry nudged Jazz. "I'm sorry our project stinks because of me," he repeated.

Then he inched over next to Rocky. "I'm sorry I acted like such a jerk on the tennis court," he said. "You totally played your best."

Rocky shrugged like it didn't matter.

Henry didn't know what else to do. He had said he was sorry. He hoped Rocky wouldn't stay mad forever.

At home, Henry spaced his trophies so there wasn't a hole anymore. Why had he made such a big deal about wanting another one? Or about playing more matches?

Would Rocky ever play *any*

sport with him, ever again? Would anybody?

"Henry!" called his mom. "Your friends are out-side."

Henry flew down the stairs, tore through the kitchen door, and cleared his back steps in one giant leap.

"Want to shoot some hoops?" asked Rocky. He held a basketball against one hip.

"Yeah!" cried Henry. He didn't even try to reverse his smile muscles. "How about three on two? Rocky and me against the rest of you." He swept his arm wide to include Rita, Jazz, and Goose.

"Sure," said Jazz.

Goose shrugged, then nodded.

"We'll destroy you," said Rita.

"No way," said Rocky. He dribbled the ball—one, two, three times. He heaved the ball into the air.

Swish! The ball dropped through the net as if it had eyes.

"Yes!" exclaimed Henry.

Rita grabbed the ball, backed up a few steps, then went in for a layup. "Two points!" she cried, twirling like a dancer.

"N'uh-uh," said Henry. "You didn't take it out of bounds first."

"I did too."

"You did not."

Henry snatched up the ball and fired a bounce pass to Rocky. Goose stepped in and stole it.

"Don't worry," said Rocky, waving his hands in Goose's face. "I've got it."

Henry ran to get open under the basket.

Henry knew he was lucky. He had four friends. And they liked him even when he messed up.